I LOVE VALENTINE'S DAY!

Happy Valentine's Day
Love,
Mrs. Porretta
Mrs. Barnett
Mrs. Wood

2013

Library of Congress Cataloging-in-Publication Data is available.

ISBN-13: 978-0-545-13475-0
ISBN-10: 0-545-13475-7

12 11 10 9 8 7 6 5 4 3 10 11 12 13 14 15/0

Printed in the U.S.A. 40 • First printing, January 2010

I LOVE VALENTINE'S DAY!

by Hans Wilhelm

SCHOLASTIC INC.
New York Toronto London Auckland
Sydney Mexico City New Delhi Hong Kong

It's Valentine's Day.
Look at all these cards.

LOVE
I U

Everyone got a card except me.

Maybe they forgot about me.

Nobody loves me.

Wait! That's not true!
Everyone is loved.

The rocks love me.

The flowers love me, too.

Even the snow loves me.

These tree branches love me.

All the clouds love me.

This is the best Valentine's Day ever!

Happy Valentine's Day, Kitty!

Everyone is loved—
even grouchy pussycats.

Thank you, Kitty.
I love you, too.

You are my favorite Valentine!